John Critchley Prince

Autumn leaves

Original poems

John Critchley Prince

Autumn leaves
Original poems

ISBN/EAN: 9783337206314

Printed in Europe, USA, Canada, Australia, Japan

Cover: Foto ©Andreas Hilbeck / pixelio.de

More available books at **www.hansebooks.com**

AUTUMN LEAVES.

Original Poems.

BY

JOHN CRITCHLEY PRINCE,

AUTHOR OF "HOURS WITH THE MUSES," "DREAMS AND REALITIES,"
"POETIC ROSARY," ETC.

NEW EDITION, WITH ADDITIONAL POEMS.

A simple robin warbling on the spray,
Unenvious of the lark that hails the day,
Yet glad and thankful if his humble strain
Cheer one sad soul—charm one lorn heart from pain.

LONDON: SIMPKIN, MARSHALL & CO.,
STATIONERS' HALL COURT.

MANCHESTER: ABEL HEYWOOD & SON,
56 AND 58 OLDHAM STREET.
1866.

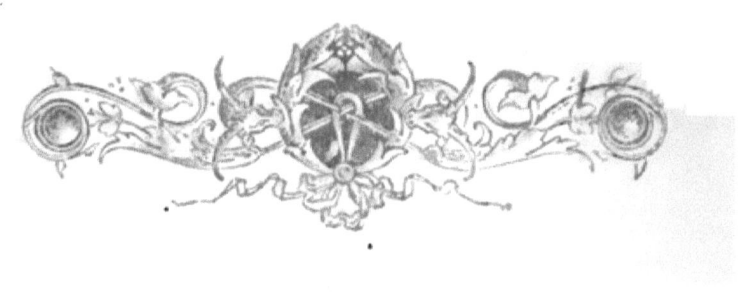

DEDICATORY SONNET.

TO whom shall I devote, with love and truth,
    These Autumn Leaves, in the Autumn of my days,
    These well intended, but imperfect lays—
But unto thee, my faithful, patient Ruth !
Thy heart received me in my noblest hour,
    And in my weakest did not cast me out,
But clung to me with sympathising power,
    And fenced me with affection round about.
'Mid poverty, and hunger, and despair,
    We grieved and suffered, but divided not,
And still we tremble 'neath oppressive care,
    But to the end we 'll bear one common lot.
Preserve in memory of our troubled past
These voices of my song—perchance the last.

CONTENTS.

A BOOK FOR THE HOME FIRESIDE.

WHEN the night cometh round, and our duties are
    done,
    And a calm stealeth over the breast,
When the bread that is needful is honestly won,
    And our worldly thoughts nestle to rest,—
How sweet at that hour is the truth-written page,
    With fancy and fiction allied !
The magic of childhood, the solace of age,
    Is a Book for the Home Fireside.

There manhood may strengthen a wavering mind
    By the sage's severest of lore ;
There woman, with sweetness and pathos combined,
    Make the fountains of feeling run o'er ;
There the voices of children may warble like birds
    What the poet has uttered with pride,
And the faint and despairing take heart at the words
    Of a Book for the Home Fireside.

Many minds have been trained into goodness and grace,
    And many stern hearts chastened down ;
Many men have been nerved to look up with bright face,
    Whatever misfortune might frown ;
Many souls have been roused to new life, and grown
    Though baffled, obstructed, and tried ;   [great,
Have been schooled to endure, taught to "labour and
       wait,"
    By a Book for the Home Fireside.

And not with the presence of Home is it gone,
    For abroad in the fulness of day
Its spirit remains with us, cheering us on
    O'er the roughness of life's common way ;
And nature is lovely, but lovelier yet
    Through the glass of reflection descried ;
We have read of her wonders—and who would forget ?—
    In a Book for the Home Fireside.

Whate'er be my fortune, in shadow or shine,—
    'Mid comfort, stern labour, or woe,
May I ne'er miss the taste of those waters divine
    From the well-springs of Genius that flow ;
I should lose a sweet charm, I should lack a great joy,
    And my heart would seem withered and dried,
Did I want what has been my delight from a boy,—
    A Book for the Home Fireside.

Bless the Bards and the Prosemen, wherever their clime,
    Who bequeath us the wealth of their thought,
Their true revelations, their visions sublime,
    Their fancies so tenderly wrought !

We were poor, with the riches of kings for our dower,
  Without what their pens have supplied ;
And that brain must be barren which owns not the power
  Of a Book for the Home Fireside.

Dear child ! let thy leisure be linked with the page,
  But one nor too light nor austere ;
May its precepts improve thee, its spirit engage,
  And its sentiments soften and cheer ;
May it keep thy affections in freshness and bloom ;
  Console thee, exalt thee, and guide ;
Be a flower in the sunshine, a star in the gloom,
  A Book for the Home Fireside !

AUTUMNAL SONNETS.

IT seems but yesterday, when merry Spring
   Leapt o'er the lea, while clustering round her feet
   Sprang buds and blossoms, beautiful and sweet,
And her glad voice made wood and welkin ring.
Now Autumn lords it o'er the quiet lands,
   Like Joseph, clad in many-coloured vest,
Flinging rich largess from his bounteous hands,
   And calling upon man to be his guest.
Like Joseph, he dispenses needful corn,
   And fruitage, too, of many a goodly tree,
So that we may not feel ourselves forlorn,
   Pining for sustenance at Nature's knee.
Corn, oil, and wine! there's music in the sound!
Oh, would that none might lack when such blest gifts
     abound!

Not yet is Autumn desolate and cold,
   For all his woods are kindling into hues
Of gorgeous beauty, mixed and manifold,
   Which in the soul a kindred glow transfuse.

The stubble fields gleam out like tarnished gold
   In the mild lustre of the temperate day,
And where the ethereal ocean is unrolled,
   Light clouds, like barques of silver, float alway,
Ruffling the colours of the forest leaves,
   The winds make music as they come and go ;
Whispers the withering brake ; the streamlet grieves,
   Or seems to grieve, with a melodious woe ;
Whilst in soft notes, which o'er the heart prevail,
The ruddy-breasted Robin pours his tender tale.

The varying seasons ever roll, and run
   Into each other, like that arc of light,
Born of the shower and coloured by the sun—
   Which spans the heavens when April skies are bright.
First comes green-kirtled Spring, who leadeth on
   Blue-mantled Summer of maturer age,
Sultana of the year.   When she is gone,
   Gold-girdled Autumn, solemn as a sage,
Reigns for a time, and on earth's ample page
   (Illumined by his hand) writes " Plenty here !"
Then white-cowled Winter steps upon the stage,
   Like aged monk, keen, gloomy, and austere.
But he whose soul sustains no cloud nor thrall,
Perceives power, beauty, good, and fitness in them all

THE CHILD AND THE DEW-DROPS.

(IN MEMORY OF A LOST SON.)

"O DEAREST mother! tell me, pray,
　　Why are the dew-drops gone so soon?
　Could they not stay till close of day,
　To sparkle on the flowery spray,
　　Or on the fields till noon?"

The mother gazed upon her boy,
　Earnest with thought beyond his years,
And felt a sharp and sad annoy,
That meddled with her deepest joy,
　But she restrained her tears.

"My child, 'tis said such beauteous things,
　Too often loved with vain excess,
Are swept away by angel wings,
Before contamination clings
　To their frail loveliness.

" Behold yon rainbow, brightening yet,
  To which all mingled hues are given !
There are thy dew-drops, grandly set
In a resplendent coronet
  Upon the brow of heaven.

" No stain of earth can reach them there,
  Woven with sunbeams there they shine,
A transient vision of the air,
But yet a symbol, pure and fair,
  Of love and peace divine."

The boy gazed upward into space,
  With eager and inquiring eyes,
While o'er his fair and thoughtful face
Came a faint glory, and a grace
  Transmitted from the skies.

Ere the last odorous sigh of May,
  That child lay down beneath the sod ;
Like dew, his young soul passed away,
To mingle with the brighter day
  That veils the throne of God.

Mother, thy fond, foreboding heart
  Truly foretold thy loss and pain,
But thou didst choose the patient part
Of resignation to the smart,
  And owned thy loss his gain.

MERCY.

GOD looked, and smiled, upon the wakening earth,
  In form, power, motion, wond'rous and complete—
Which in the flush and beauty of new birth
  Breasted the seas of ether at His feet.
Forth with companion worlds, that throbbed and shone
With warmth and light transmitted from His throne,
On noiseless axles ever spinning round,
She took her radiant way along the vast profound.

God called to Him three ministers, who wait
  Unceasing on His wise and sovereign will,
Servants, and yet partakers of His state,
  And watchers of all human good and ill ;
An angel-formed triumvirate, with air
Of lofty thought beaming from foreheads bare,
August in presence and they were in name,
And clothed in flowing robes of many-coloured flame.

Justice was one, in aspect calm and cold,
  With a severe, but not oppressive mien ;
Another Truth, with brow sublimely bold,
  And onward looks, all radiant and serene ;

The last was Mercy, whose consoling eyes
Caught the reflection of celestial skies,
Mercy, with beauteous and beseeching face,
And wedded hands upraised with supplicating grace.

" Let us make Man, for, lo ! yon lovely sphere,
　Which in its amplitude of orbit rolls,
Shall be—ye bright Intelligences, hear !—
　Place of probation for immortal souls ;
There shall man dwell—there shall he rule and reign,
But not exempt from sinfulness and pain,
Yet destined, 'mid his troubles and his storms,
To people boundless Heaven with countless angel forms."

"Oh, make him not !" cried Justice ; " I foresee
　That he will trample on Thy sacred laws,
Doubt, question, violate Thy great decree,
　Feel his own being, yet deny its cause."
"Oh, make him not !" cried Truth ; "for he will toil
'Gainst Thee and me, and ruthlessly despoil
Thy sanctuaries, grow corrupt and vain,
Worship himself, and scorn Thy everlasting reign."

" Create this being, good and gracious Lord !"
　Said gentle Mercy, with imploring look—
"And I will guide him by Thy precious Word,
　The wisdom of Thy yet unwritten Book ;
My voice shall move him with mysterious power ;
My wings shall shield him in the perilous hour ;
I'll check, subdue, inspire, as best I may,
The soul thou deign'st to breathe into the form of clay."

" Even so be it !" And man straightway was born,
   Richly endued, and full of love and trust ;
Serene, pure, happy, was his early morn,
   Till the dread Tempter bowed him to the dust ;
Then shame, and sorrow, and recurrent sin
Shook his best nature, soiled the shrine within ;
But Mercy pleaded, and God sent him light
To cheer his darkling soul, and guide his steps aright.

Let's take the angel Mercy to our heart,
   And with her walk the rugged paths of life ;
List to her teachings ; learn the exalted art
   That conquers hatred, prejudice, and strife.
Not Truth, nor Justice, must we put away,
But lean towards Mercy whensoe'er we may ;
Forgive our brother, be ourselves forgiven,
And thus by gentlest deeds sue for the smiles of Heaven.

A PLEA FOR WOMAN.

IT is well that beauteous woman
  Has the quickest sense of wrong;
That the tenderest traits of feeling
  To her faithful heart belong;
That her pure, heroic spirit,
  Made to soften and prevail,
Win their way to truth and justice,
  When our ruder efforts fail.

Has she not from earliest ages
  Borne the heaviest load of life,
Suffer'd in the silent conflict,
  Struggled in the rudest strife?
Has she not with patient meekness
  Won and worn the martyr's crown?
Even by her seeming weakness
  Pulled the strongest tyrant down?

Day by day she has encountered
  In her own domestic round,
Sharpest griefs, severest tortures,
  All for language too profound;

Trembled through her woman's nature
  Lest the outward world should know,
Single in her calm endurance,
  Loving in her lofty woe.

Pestilence has not appalled her,
  Dungeons have not driven her back,
She has smiled upon the scaffold,
  And been silent on the rack.
She, a ministress of mercy,
  Has gone forth from door to door,
Suaging sickness, soothing sorrow,
  In the chambers of the poor.

All unselfish, she has pleaded,
  With an angel's earnest grace,
'Gainst the brand-mark and the bondage
  Of old Afric's dusky race ;
And not only for the alien,
  If an alien there can be—
But for all who shrink and suffer
  On her own side of the sea.

Pleaded for her sister woman,
  Moiling through the joyless day,
Hungering, hopeless, ever trembling
  Lest she swerve from virtue's way ;
Pleaded for the little children
  Growing up to dangerous youth,
For the want of wholesome knowledge,
  For the lack of genial truth

And she has not been ungifted
  With the mind's superior powers,
But has brought us bloom and fragrance
  From the muse's magic bowers ;
She has stirred our inmost natures
  With a true and graceful pen,
Even snatched a wreath of honour
  From the bolder brows of men.

Then let this dear mediator,
  This companion of our way,
Have her natural power and province
  In the great work of to-day ;
Let her go upon her mission,
  If she have no wish to roam,
Nor to break the ties that bind her
  To the sacred bounds of home.

Let her have the purest knowledge,
  That hereafter she may be
Teacher of serenest virtues,
  To the children round her knee ;
Foresight, faithfulness, forbearance,
  Charity, and all good things,
Which prepare the human creature
  For its future angel wings.

HOME.

LET us honour the gods of the household alway,
  Love ever the hearth and its graces,
The spot where serenely and cheerfully play
  The smiles of familiar faces ;
Where the calm, tender tones of affection are heard ;
  Where the child's gladsome carol is ringing ;
Where the heart's best emotions are quickened and stirred,
  By the founts that are inwardly springing.

Oh ! what are the charms of the banquet-hour glee,
  And the words of frivolity spoken,
To the holier joys 'neath our quiet roof-tree,
  When the compact of love is unbroken ?
Not the selfish delight, the obstreperous mirth,
  Not the glare of conventional splendour,
May compare with the spells that encircle our hearth,
  If it hold but the true and the tender.

Too long 'mid the gay revel's profitless scene
  The weak one may foolishly linger,
Where false pleasure lures him with treacherous mien,
  And holds him with magical finger ;

But he who has wisdom to baffle the snare
    Clings close to his home, and how dearly !
Fond feelings, kind looks, are in store for him there,
    And gentle words uttered sincerely.

Howsoever the spirit may struggle and fret
    In the conflict of worldly commotion,
There's a solace to soothe and to strengthen us yet,
    If home have our truest devotion.
It needeth not hall, nor palatial dome,
    To afford us a refuge so holy ;
To the loving and pure any spot is a home,
    Be it ever so narrow and lowly.

And home, when it *is* home, sounds sweet in our ears,
    For it speaks of our heart-cherished treasure ;
'Tis a word which beguiles us of tenderest tears,
    Or thrills us with tranquillest pleasure ;
It prompts us to set rude enjoyments at nought,
    It chastens our speech and demeanour ;
It nerves us to action, awakes us to thought,
    And makes our whole being serener.

Dear home, rightly guarded and graced, is a soil
    Where the virtues are constantly growing ;
'Tis a sanctified shelter, the guerdon of toil,
    A thousand calm blessings bestowing.
Home, country, humanity, heaven !   How they please,
    Things leaving all else at a distance !
Who lends a true soul, does his duty to these,
    Fulfils the best ends of existence.

LOOK UP.

"LOOK up!" cried the seaman, with nerves
       like steel,
   As skyward his glance he cast,
And beheld his own son grow giddy, and reel
  On the point of the tapering mast.
Look up! and the bold boy lifted his face,
  And banished his brief alarms,
Slid down at once from his perilous place,
  And leapt in his father's arms.

Look up! we cry to the sorely oppressed,
  Who seem from all comfort shut,
You had better look up to the mountain crest,
  Than down to the precipice foot.
The one offers heights ye may hope to gain,
  Pure ether, and freedom, and room;
The other bewilders the aching brain
  With roughness, and danger, and gloom.

Look up! meek soul, by affliction bent,
  Nor dally with dull despair,
Look up, and with faith, to the firmament,
  For Heaven and mercy are there.

The frail flower droops in the stormy shower,
  And the shadows of needful night,
But it looks to the sun in the after hour,
  And takes full measure of light.

Look up! sad man, by adversity brought
  From high unto low estate
Play not with the bane of corrosive thought,
  Nor murmur at chance and fate.
Renew thy hopes ; look the world in the face,
  For it helps not those who repine ;
Press on, and its cheer will amend thy pace ;
  Succeed, and its homage is thine.

Look up ! great crowd, who are foremost set
  In the changeful battle of life ;
Some days of calm may reward ye yet
  For years of allotted strife.
Look up, and *beyond*, there's a guerdon there
  For the humble and pure of heart,
Fruition of joys unalloyed by care,
  Of peace that can never depart.

Look up ! large spirit, by Heaven inspired,
  Thou rare and expansive soul !
Look up, with endeavour and zeal untired,
  And strive for the loftiest goal ;
Advance, and encourage the kindred throng,
  Who toil up the slopes behind,
To follow, and hail with triumphant song
  The holier regions of mind !

NOTHING IS LOST.

NOTHING is lost; the drop of dew
　　That trembles on the leaf or flower
Is but exhaled, to fall anew
　　In summer's thunder shower :
Perchance to shine within the bow
　　That fronts the sun at fall of day ;
Perchance to sparkle in the flow
　　Of fountains far away.

Nought lost, for even the tiniest seed,
　　By wild birds borne or breezes blown,
Finds something suited to its need,
　　Wherein 'tis sown and grown ;
Perchance finds sustenance and soil
　　In some remote and desert place,
Or 'mid the crowded homes of toil
　　Sheds usefulness and grace.

The little drift of common dust,
　　By the March winds disturbed and tossed,
Though scattered by the fitful gust,
　　Is changed, but never lost ;

It yet may bear some sturdy stem,
  Some proud oak battling with the blast,
Or crown with verdurous diadem
  Some ruin of the past.

The furnace quenched, the flame put out,
  Still cling to earth or soar in air,
Transformed, diffused, or blown about,
  To burn again elsewhere ;
Haply to make the beacon-blaze
  That gleams athwart the briny waste,
Or light the social lamp, whose rays
  Illume the home of taste.

The touching tones of minstrel art,
  The breathings of some mournful flute,
(Which we have heard with listening heart,)
  Are not extinct when mute ;
The language of some household song ;
  The perfume of some cherished flower,
Though gone from outward sense, belong
  To memory's after hour.

So with our words, or harsh, or kind,
  Uttered, they are not all forgot,
But leave some trace upon the mind,
  Pass on, yet perish not.
As they are spoken, so they fall
  Upon the spirit spoken to,
Scorch it like drops of burning gall,
  Or soothe like honey dew.

So with our deeds, for good or ill
    They have their power, scarce understood :
Then let us use our better will
    To make them rife with good.
Like circles on a lake they go,
    Ring within ring, and never stay ;
Oh, that our deeds were fashioned so
    That they might bless away.

Then since these lesser things ne'er die,
    But work beyond our poor control,
Say, shall that suppliant for the sky,
    The greater human soul ?
Ah, no ! it yet will spurn the past,
    And search the future for its rest,
Joyful, if it be found at last
    'Mong the redeemed and blest !

LOVE.

LOVE is an odour from the heavenly bowers
    Which stirs our senses tenderly, and brings
        Dreams which are shadows of diviner things,
Beyond this grosser atmosphere of ours.
An oasis of verdure and of flowers,
    Love smileth on the pilgrim's weary way ;
    There sweeter airs, there fresher waters play ;
There purer solace speeds the tranquil hours.
This glorious passion, unalloyed, endowers
    With moral beauty all who feel its fires ;
    Maid, wife and offspring, sister, mother, sire,
Are names and symbols of its hallowed powers.
Love is immortal, from our hold may fly
Earth's other joys, but Love can never die.

THE RETURN OF PEACE.

ONCE more to visit a distracted world,
  The spirit of sweet Peace comes trembling down,
War's ensanguined flag is newly furled,
  And the gorged vulture from his banquet flown ;
She comes to solace our lorn hearts again
  For countless losses in the fatal fray ;
Oh, let us give her an enduring reign,
  Nor scare the angel visitant away !

Her deeds are bloodless, dignified, and just,
  'Gainst the mixed evils of our lower life,
And far more worthy of our hopeful trust
  Than the vain victories of mortal strife ;
Against injustice, ignorance, and crime,
  She sets her hallowed powers in bright array ;
Oh, let us make her sojourn here sublime,
  Nor scare the angel visitant away.

Let stalwart Labour clear his clouded brow,
  Toil on, but with strong rectitude of soul,
Seize manfully the treasures of the *Now*,
  And strive with honour for a loftier goal ;

Let him love Freedom, whose refulgent wings
   Add richer glory to the glorious day,
And Peace, for the calm blessings that she brings,
   Nor scare the angel visitant away.

Let men who make or minister the laws,
   So use them that the humblest may rejoice,
And get the noble meed of pure applause
   From a united people's grateful voice ;
Let them give lustre, majesty, and grace,
   And vital spirit, to the lands they sway,
Keep faith with Peace, and bless her dear embrace,
   Nor scare the angel visitant away.

Art, Science, Knowledge, may serenely grow,
   And human virtues quicken and expand,
Even gaunt poverty o'ercome its woe,
   Where Peace remains the guardian of the land ;
But he is wilful, pitiless, or blind,
   From right, and righteous feeling, all astray,
Foe to his God, his country, and his kind,
   Who scares the angel visitant away.

For dormant passion, prejudice, and pride,
   Start into evil at War's trumpet-call ;
And hearts are seared ; and souls are trouble-tried,
   And minds subjected to a slavish thrall.
While industry is baffled, Waste runs wild,
   And Liberty stands still in mute dismay !
Let us choose Peace, if wise and undefiled,
   Nor scare the angel visitant away.

Albeit men differ in their clime and creed,
　In thought and predilection, as in tongue,
Say, would the nations murmur to be freed
　From hideous War and its unfailing wrong?
Would they could bid the mighty torment cease,
　By some great law which none would disobey,
Make an inviolate covenant with Peace,
　Nor scare the angel visitant away.

SAINT CHRISTOPHER.

A LEGEND.

" MY limbs wax strong, my thoughts expand,"
    Said Christopher of old,
  As he lay musing 'mid the hills,
    His flock within the fold,—
" I fain would serve some mighty power,
  The highest, if may be,
And change this dull and dreamy life
  For one more wide and free."

He girt his robe about his loins,
  And wandered far away,
Until he reached a battle-ground,
  That shuddered with the fray.
With stalwart strength, and dauntless heart,
  He turned the tide of fight,
And snatched a wreath of victory
  Ere waned the evening light.

Then the exulting host bowed down
    Before a gorgeous shrine,
And seemed to offer words of praise
    Unto a Power divine.
"A king divine?" said Christopher,
    "Where does the monarch dwell?"
"Above, beyond us," answered they,
    "But where we cannot tell."

Again he gathered up his robe,
    And donned his sandal shoes,
Took staff in hand, and wandered forth,
    Not knowing where to choose;
Until amid the lonesome wild
    He met a hermit hoar,
Who lifted up his kindly eyes,
    And scanned him o'er and o'er.

"Where may I find the king divine?"
    Outspoke the pilgrim brave,
"I fain would serve him with my strength,
    More truly than a slave."
"His kingdom is not here, my son,
    Albeit his cross I wear.
Wouldst win admission to his throne?
    Lift up thy voice in prayer."

"I cannot pray, thou reverent man,
    I have not words enow,
But if brave deeds may aught avail,
    These will I strive to do."

" Behold yon torrent !" said the sage,
  " That roars from hill to glen ;
Wait on its banks, and watch for work ;
  Serve God by helping men."

The pilgrim found a leafy tent
  Beside that dangerous wave,
And daily sought, with earnest zeal,
  To succour and to save ;
And when he snatched some precious life
  From that o'erwhelming stream,
His good, glad feelings found their way
  Up to the great Supreme.

One day there came a little child,
  With soft and sunny hair,
With eyes that beamed serenely mild,
  With face divinely fair ;
And with a voice of winning power
  The little stranger cried—
" Come help me, valiant Christopher,
  Across this angry tide."

He took the lovely infant up
  Upon his shoulders broad,
With strange emotions in his soul,
  That pleased, yet overawed ;
But fiercer grew the torrent's force,
  And heavier grew the child,
Who almost bowed the strong man down
  Beneath those waters wild.

" O river ! why dost rave the more
　　In absence of the storm ?
And, child, what art thou that I bend
　　Beneath thy tiny form ? "
" Press on, good servant as thou art,
　　Be faithful to thy word ;
Thou bear'st the world's whole weight to-day,
　　For I am Christ, thy Lord."

" The stream is passed, the danger o'er,
　　Blest be thy future powers !
Here plant thy staff.　Behold how soon
　　It blossoms into flowers !
There let it stand and flourish long,
　　A symbol and a sign
Of thy unswerving faithfulness
　　Unto the King divine."

" Unsought, untaught of men, thy heart,
　　Moved by a hidden power,
Did scorn the specious things of earth
　　For Heaven's transcending dower.
I give thee speech, that thou may'st teach
　　Hearts kindred to thy own ;
Go forth, and bring repentant souls
　　Unto my Father's throne."

Prone on the earth, Saint Christopher
　　His trembling homage paid,
While on his head the holy child
　　A lasting blessing laid.

When he looked up, the vision fair
  Had vanished from his eyes,
But an unwonted glory streamed
  Along the wondering skies.

THE LOST ONE.

I MOURN, albeit I mourn in vain,
    To miss that being from my side
Who bound in Love's resistless chain
    My selfishness and pride ;
She whom I proved in after days
    A faultless friend, a faithful wife,
Who cheered me through the roughest ways
    Along the vale of life.

I miss her greeting when I rise
    To needful toil at early morn,
And the bright welcome of her eyes
    When irksome day is worn ;
I sorely miss from ear and sight
    Her comely face, her gentle tongue,
Which praised me when I went aright.
    And warned when I was wrong.

I lack her love, which filled my heart
    With kindred tenderness and joy,
And fondly kept my soul apart
    From the harsh world's annoy

That love which raised me from the dust
   Of sordid wish and low desire,
And taught me by its own sweet trust
   How nobly to aspire.

My hopes were wilder than I deemed,
   When she espoused my humble lot,
For my connubial pleasures seemed
   As they would perish not ;
But an unerring Providence,
   Whose power is ever just and great,
Called my beloved companion hence,
   And left me desolate.

The greenness from my path is gone,
   Its springs are sunken in the sand,
And wearily I travel on
   Across a desert land.
The horizon round me, once so bright
   With glorious hues, seems dim and bare
But the far distance shows one light
   Which keeps me from despair.

Oh, no ! not wholly desolate,
   For she has left her image here,
And I will wrestle with my fate
   For sake of one so dear.
Great God, keep strong and undefiled
   The only fledgeling in my nest,
My winsome boy, my only child,
   And make his father blest.

May his lost mother's spirit now
　　Look down from her exalted place,
And shed on his unconscious brow
　　A portion of her grace!
May Heaven inspire my widowed soul
　　For highest duties, holiest things,
And when I near the shadowy goal
　　Lend me immortal wings.

NOT BREAD ALONE.

ALBEIT for lack of bread we die,
  Die in a hundred nameless ways,
   'Tis not for bread alone we cry
    In these our later days.

It is not fit that man should spend
  His strength of frame, his length of years,
In toiling for that daily end,
  Mere bread, oft wet with tears.

That is not wholly good and gain
  Which seals the mind and scars the heart,
The life-long labour to sustain
  Man's perishable part.

His is the need and his the right
  Of leisure, free from harsh control,
That he may seek for mental light,
  And cultivate his soul.

C

Leisure to foster into bloom
 Affections struggling to expand ;
And make his thought, with ampler room,
 Refine his skill of hand.

And he should look with reverent eyes
 On Nature's ever-varying page ;
Not solely are the wondrous skies
 For schoolman and for sage.

Earth's flower-hues blush, heaven's star-lights burn,
 Not only for the easy few ;
To them the toiling man should turn
 For truth and pleasure too.

And he should have his proper share
 Of God's great gifts, whate'er they be,
Food, raiment, stainless light and air,
 And knowledge pure and free.

But if ye stint his brain or bread,
 And drive him in one dreary round,
(Since he and his must needs be fed,)
 Ye crush him to the ground.

His mind can have no soaring wing ;
 His heart can feel no generous glow ;
Ye make of him that wretched thing—
 A slave, and yet a foe !

THE HOUSEHOLD DARLING.

LITTLE Ella, fairest, dearest
    Unto me and unto mine,
   Earthly cherub, coming nearest
    Unto me and unto mine !
Her brief absence frets and pains me,
  Her blithe presence solace brings,
Her spontaneous love restrains me
  From a hundred selfish things.

Little Ella moveth lightly,
  Like a graceful fawn at play ;
Like a brooklet running brightly
  In the genial smile of May :
Like a breeze upon the meadows,
  All besprent with early flowers ;
Like a bird 'mid sylvan shadows,
  In the golden summer hours.

You should see her, when with Nature
  She goes forth to think or play,
Every limb and every feature
  Drinking in the joy of day ;

Stooping oft 'mid floral splendour,
　　Snatching colours and perfumes,
She doth seem, so fair and tender,
　　Kin to the ambrosial blooms.

Sweet thought sitteth like a garland
　　On her placid brows and eyes,
Eyes which seem to see a far land
　　Through the intervening skies ; .
And she seems to listen often
　　To some voice beyond the spheres,
Whilst her earnest features soften
　　Into calmness, kin to tears.

Not all mirthful is her manner,
　　Though no laugh so blithe as hers ;
Grave demeanour comes upon her
　　When her inmost nature stirs.
When a gentle lip reproves her,
　　All her gladsome graces flee,
But the word " forgiveness " moves her
　　With new confidence and glee.

Should a shade of sickness near me,
　　Then she takes a holier grace,
Comes to strengthen and to cheer me
　　With her angel light of face.
Up the stair I hear her coming,
　　Duly at the morning hour,
Softly singing, sweetly humming,
　　Like a bee about a flower.

Good books wake serenest feelings
　In her undeveloped mind,
Holy thoughts, whose high revealings
　Teach her love for human kind.
Music thrills her with a fervour
　As from songs of seraphim ;
May bright spirits teach and nerve her
　To partake their perfect hymn !

We will show her things of beauty
　In the purest form and hue,
And the charms of moral duty,
　Though our virtues are but few ;
We will strive, despite our weakness,
　So to train her thoughts and deeds
That true firmness, linked with meekness,
　May sustain her when she needs.

God of heaven ! in Thy good seeing
　Spare this darling child to me,
Spare me this unsullied being
　Till she bring me close to Thee !
Unseen angels ! bless her, mould her
　Into goodness, clothed with grace,
That at last I may behold her
　Talking with ye, face to face !

THE DRUMMER'S DEATH-ROLL.

TO a region of song and of sunnier day,
 The battle-host wended its wearisome way,
  Through the terrible Splugen's tenebrious gloom,
That seemed to lead on to the portals of doom.
But the Alp-spirit struggled to break and to bar
The resolute march of those minions of war ;
For the savage winds howled through the gorges of stone ;
And the pine forest muttered a menace and moan ;
And the rush of the hurricane caused them to reel ;
And the frost-breezes smote them like sabres of steel ;
And the torrents incessantly thundered and hissed ;
And the scream of the eagle came harsh through the
  mist ;
And the avalanche stirred with a deep, muffled roar,
Like the boom of the sea on a desolate shore,
Till it leapt from its throne with a flash, and a speed
That hurled to destruction both rider and steed;
And Love could not hope, by the strongest endeavour,
To weep on the spot where they slumber for ever !

A drummer went down with the burden of snow,*
But struggled, and lived, 'mid the buried below,
Survived for a brief, but how awful a space !
In the granite-bound depth of that horrible place.
He looked from the jaws of that rock-riven grave,
And called on the Mother of Jesus to save ;
But Heaven seemed deaf to his piteous wail,
And men could not hear his sad voice on the gale ;
And, alas ! human help could not come to him there,
Nor the breezes waft home the farewell of his prayer.
But still he clung closely to hope and to life,
And waged with disaster a desperate strife,—
A conflict which midnight might solemnly close,
And leave him the peace of a lasting repose.

A sudden thought thrilled through his wandering
    brain,
His drum lay beside him, he smote it amain,
And brought from its hollow a vigorous sound,
That wakened the wild mountain echoes around,
And startled the vulture that circled away,
But returned to his vigil, impatient for prey.
Roll, roll went the drum till the sunset was passed,
And scattered its tones on the hurrying blast,
While his friends, far away on their Alpine career,
Caught the dolorous sound with a sorrowful ear ;

* In the passage of Macdonald through the frightful region of the
Splugen, one of the drummers having been shot in a snow-bank from the
avalanche into a frightful gulf, and having struggled forth alive, but out of
sight and reach of his comrades, was heard beating his drum for several
hours in the abyss, vainly expecting rescue. There was no reaching him,
and Death with icy fingers stilled the roll of the drum, and beat out the last
pulsations of hope and life in his bosom.—*Pilgrim in the Jungfrau.*

For they knew that a comrade was hopelessly lost,
Left alone to the tortures of hunger and frost,
Cut off from the reach of humanity there,
And beating his drum with the strength of despair!

But who can imagine his quick-coming fears,
His visions, his agonies, yearnings, and tears,
When paralysed, spent, and benumbed to the bone,
He sank on his snow-bed to perish alone ?
What fancy can bring back the pictures that passed
O'er the brain of the desolate lost one at last,
Ere death came to still the last pulse in his breast,
And stretch out his limbs in a petrified rest ?

Perchance his bright childhood came back to his
thought
And his youth, when his heart in love's meshes was
caught,
And his village, embowered in a vine-covered vale,
With peace in its aspect, and health in its gale ;
The blithe peasant maiden he learned to adore,
And his home which his shadow would darken no
more,
That home where his parents and kindred were gay,
In the hope of his coming at no distant day,
That meeting which never would gladden their eyes,
Save in the blest climate of holier skies.

Whate'er his last hope, aspiration, and prayer,
Untended, he died in his loneliness there,
In a place of sublimities, horrors, and storms,
Surrounded by Nature's most terrible forms,

Where the voices of avalanche, wild wind and wave,
Sang a varying dirge o'er his rock-riven grave.
Let us hope that his soul, in the hour of its gloom,
By its faith cast aside all the terrors of doom,
Left the desolate dust to commix with the clod,
And awakened with joy in the regions of God!

LEONORE.

OH, for a day of that departed time
  When thou and I, lost Leonore, were young!
That dawn of feeling, that delicious prime
  When Hope sang for us an unceasing song!
When Life was love, and love was joy unworn,
  And clouds turned all their silver to our gaze;
When each sweet night brought forth a sweeter morn!
  Where art thou, dearest of my early days?

Oh, what a world of poesy was ours,
  And poesy with passion undefiled!
Heaven with its stars, and earth with all her flowers
  Seemed made for us, for us alone they smiled.
Fused in each other's dreams, a constant spring,
  One, yet apart, we trod all pleasant ways;
Sat down with Nature, heard her teach and sing:
  Where art thou, dearest of my early days?

With thee, all beauty wore a lovelier face,
  With thee, all grandeur a sublimer mien,
With thee, all music had a holier grace,
  With thee, all motion ecstasy unseen ;
Without thee, life was colourless and vain,
  And common pleasure a bewildering maze,
All thought was languor, and all effort pain ;—
  Where art thou, dearest of my early days ?

I loved, how well let this worn cheek attest,
  And those sad eyes, with fresh tears streaming o'er ;
Deep in the hidden chambers of my breast
  The fire burns on, but ne'er to bless me more !
Oh, *nevermore !* a dreary word that falls
  Like a dread knell that sets the brain acraze,
A word of doom that withers and appals !
  Where art thou, dearest of my early days ?

We loved, but one with unrelenting power,
  With selfish soul intent on cruel schemes,
Stepped in between us one disastrous hour,
  And swept to ruin all our hopes and dreams ;
And we were parted—thou to share the life
  Of the gay crowd that dazzles and betrays ;
I to contend with penury and strife ;—
  Where art thou, dearest of my early days ?

I see thee as I saw thee long ago,
  (A fond, yet fatal time for thee and me !)
When with the eloquence of love and woe
  We blest each other 'neath the hawthorn tree :

The ancient hawthorn, whose entangled boughs
   Bloom where our native river sings and plays,
Which heard our earliest and our latest vows;—
   Where art thou, dearest of my early days?

I see thee as I saw when, one sweet eve,
   I dared to pour my passion in thy ear,
And thou didst lean to listen and believe,
   With mixed emotions of delight and fear.
I see the quick blush flitting o'er thy cheek,
   And the soft fire of thy confiding gaze ;
I feel thy heart in throbbing language speak,—
   Where art thou, dearest of my early days?

I see thee as I saw thee everywhere,
   In the calm household graceful, quiet, kind ;
In the broad sunshine and the breezy air
   Bright as the beam, and buoyant as the wind ;
I see thee flushed, and floating like a cloud
   In the gay festival's enchanting maze ;
And, lovelier still, in prayer serenely bowed ;—
   Where art thou, dearest of my early days?

Art thou of earth, sweet spirit of the past ?
   The lost and mourned, the adored and unforgot !
Hast thou been beaten by Misfortune's blast,
   Or dost thou revel in a brighter lot ?
Is there another whom thy eyes approve ?
   Is there another whom thy heart obeys ?
Or dost thou sorrow o'er thy blighted love ?—
   Where art thou, dearest of my early days?

Art thou of Heaven ? and dost thou now behold,
   Stooping in pity from thy sainted sphere,
Thy poor, forsaken worshipper of old,
   Despairing, desolate, and darkling here ?
I look for thee, I long for thee, I languish
   To press thee, bless thee, ere my life decays,
Still my lorn soul cries after thee with anguish,—
   Where art thou, dearest of my early days ?

TO A BLIND POET.

JUDGE me not harshly, aged man and blind,
   If in my rude, brief song, I fail to bring
   Aught worthy of thy worth.   I cannot sing
All I have seen of thy unworldly mind.
Thy clouded eyes ; thy silvery hairs ; thy kind
  And calm deep-thoughted countenance ; thy smile
  Of generous confidence, which beams midwhile
With quiet mirth, and memories unconfined ;
Thy child-like love of poetry refined ;
  Thy thirst for Nature's melodies ; thy light
  Of soul which burns behind the external night ;
Thy tolerant piety ; thy heart resigned,
Make thee a rare example, and our pride
Is humbled to behold thy blindness glorified.

GERALDINE.

THERE thou goest, there thou goest,
  In thy virgin robes arrayed,
   Pale and drooping, for thou knowest,
    What true heart thou hast betrayed.
Hark! thy bridal bells are ringing!
  Do they waken happy tears?
Their exulting peal is flinging
  Torture, discord in my ears.
Are they tuneful unto thine,
Fair and fickle Geraldine?

Now thou standest at the altar,
  Where truth only should be heard;
Dost not inly feel, and falter
  To pronounce one fateful word?
No! I hear thy lips of beauty
  Utter the degrading " yes,"
And the pastor, as in duty,
  Stretches forth his hands to bless.
Can such compact be divine,
Fair, false-hearted Geraldine?

Of the tender vows we plighted
   Thine were flung in empty air,
And my spirit is benighted
   In the darkness of despair !
Gold has bought thee ; will it bless thee ?
   Wilt thou find it ought but dross ?
Will the hands that now caress thee
   Pay thee for a true heart's loss ?
Time, perchance, will show the sign,
Fair and faithless Geraldine !

Go, and may all ill betide thee !
   Go, to splendid misery led,
With that mindless worm beside thee,—
   Him whom thou hast dared to wed !
May the ring that rounds thy finger
   Seem a serpent to thy gaze,
And a sense of loneness linger
   With thee all thy coming days ;
Loveless, childless, mayst thou pine,
Fair, false-hearted Geraldine !

Frenzied words ! I will not blame thee,
   I whose soul thy beauty won ;
Sense of duty overcame thee
   In the wrong which thou hast done.
Thou hast left a grief within me,—
   Grief which time may yet repress,
But let sweet forgiveness win me
   To desire thy happiness.
Whatsoe'er of pain be mine,
Peace be with thee, Geraldine.

THE BENIGNITY OF NATURE.

HOW beautiful is Nature, and how kind,
   In every season, every mood and dress,
    To him who woos her with an earnest mind,
   Quick to perceive and love her loveliness !
   With what a delicate, yet mighty stress,
She stills the stormy passions of the soul,
Subdues their tossings with a sweet control,
   Till each spent wave grows gradually less,
   And settles into calm !   The worldling may
Disdain her, but to me, whate'er the grief,
Whate'er the anger lingering in my breast,
   Or pain of baffled hope,—she brings relief ;
Scares the wild harpy-brood of cares away,
And to my troubled heart serenely whispers "Rest!"

Ah, yes ! the humblest of external things,
   Whereby she deigns to enchant us and to teach,
(When reverential heart the learner brings,)
   Are signs of her grand harmonies and speech.

D

The lapse of waters o'er a rugged stone ;
  A pool of reeds ; a moorland weed or flower ;
A dimpling spring ; a thorn with moss o'ergrown—
  Are symbols of her universal power.
These speak a language to the favoured sense
  Loud as the thunders, lofty as the lights
  That crowd the cope of cloudless winter nights,
And wake mute worship of Omnipotence.
Dull must he be, oppressed with earthly leaven,
Who looks on Nature's face, yet feels no nearer heaven !

CHRISTMAS EVE.

CHRISTMAS Eve came to us darkly,
   Darkly to our cottage door,
  Not with brave and boisterous greeting,
   As it used to come of yore ;
Not with soft and silent snow-fall,
  Nor with frost-wind brisk and keen,
Yet it brought its berries blushing
  'Mid the holly, hale and green.

Many busy footsteps pattered
  Through our little thoroughfare,
Children sent on pleasant errands
  For the dainties they must share ;
Young and merry-hearted maidens
  Gaily flitted to and fro,
With a quick throb in their bosoms,
  With their faces in a glow.

And the clean and cheerful windows
  Gleamed upon the sombre night,
While commingled voices, singing,
  Told of leisure and delight ;

Genial voices, linked together
  In some quaint and homely rhyme,
In some old and hopeful carol,
  Fitted for the holy time.

In that little street of workers,
  Brightening up from side to side,
One poor dwelling showed no signal
  Of the merry Christmastide ;
Feebly shone a single taper
  By the hearthstone, cold and bare ;
Poverty and tribulation
  Hung their mournful banners there.

A forlorn and friendless widow
  Gazed upon her only boy,
Whose young stream of life was ebbing
  Back unto a realm of joy ;
And as Time, with stealthy footstep,
  Strode into another day,
Death stood by that lonely mourner,
  For the life had ebbed away.

With the first burst of her anguish—
  " Hark ! what news the angels bring !"
Rang from loud and joyous voices,
  Mixed with tuneful flute and string ;
And she thought she heard her darling,
  High among the radiant spheres,
Singing with melodious gladness—
  " Mother, mother, dry thy tears !"

And she dried them, and subdued them,
    Kept their fountains sealed within,
Lest her unavailing sorrow
    Should be written down as sin ;
But the cheering faith came o'er her
    That she was not all alone,
That the Child-God of the manger
    Had the keeping of her own.

PRECIOUS TIME.

WHEN we have passed beyond life's middle arch,
   With what accelerated speed the years
     Seem to flit by us, sowing hopes and fears
As they pursue their never-ceasing march !
But is our wisdom equal to the speed
   That brings us nearer to the shadowy bourn,
   Whence me must never, never more return ?
Alas ! each wish is wiser than the deed !
" We take no note of time but from its loss,"
   Sang one who reasoned solemnly and well ;
And so it is, we make that dowry dross
   Which would be treasure, did we learn to quell
Vain dreams and passions.   Wisdom's alchemy
Transmutes to priceless gold the moments as they fly !

FORGIVENESS.

(REPRINTED BY REQUEST.)

MAN has two attendant angels
    Ever waiting at his side,
      With him wheresoe'er he wanders,
        Wheresoe'er his feet abide ;
One to warn him when he darkleth,
    And rebuke him if he stray ;
One to leave him to his nature,
    And so let him go his way.

Two recording spirits, reading
    All his life's minutest part,
Looking in his soul, and listening
    To the beatings of his heart.
Each with pen of fire electric
    Writes the good or evil wrought ;
Writes with truth that adds not, errs not,
    Purpose, action, word and thought.

One, the teacher and reprover,
 Marks each heaven-deserving deed,
Graves it with the lightning's vigour,
 Seals it with the lightning's speed ;
For the good that man achieveth,
 Good beyond an angel's doubt,
Such remains for aye and ever,
 And can not be blotted out.

One—severe and silent watcher !—
 Noteth every crime and guile,
Writes it with a holy duty,
 Seals it not, but waits awhile !
If the evil doer cry not,
 "God forgive me !" ere he sleeps,
Then the sad, stern spirit seals it,
 And the gentler spirit weeps.

To the sinner of Repentance
 Cometh soon, with healing wings,
Then the dark account is cancelled,
 And each joyful angel sings ;
While the erring one perceiveth,
 Now his troublous hour is o'er,
Music, fragrance, wafted to him
 From a yet untrodden shore.

Mild and mighty is forgiveness,
 Meekly worn if meekly won ;
Let our hearts go forth to seek it
 Ere the setting of the sun ;

Forgiveness.

Angels wait, and long to hear us
  Ask it ere the time be flown ;
Let us give it, and receive it,
  Ere the midnight cometh down.

A THOUGHT ON WAR.

'TIS strange, profanely strange, but men will stand
    Upon some spot of blighted happiness,
    Where the Omnipotent's mysterious hand
    Has fallen with disaster and distress,
And they, perchance, will question His just laws,
    Wax grave, and sigh, and look demurely wise,
As if, poor fools! they could arraign the Cause,
    And see with Wisdom's never-failing eyes!
But let them saunter o'er a battle-plain,
    Still red and reeking from the recent strife,
Where, spurred by lust of conquest and of gain,
    Relentless heels have trod out human life,
And they will prate of greatness, glory, fame!
God, how Thy creature man insults Thy holy name!

JUDGE NOT TOO HASTILY.

OH ! judge not too hastily man and his mind,
  Nor deem ye can read him at once and for aye,
There is some reservation, some secret behind
  The face that ye look upon, look as ye may.
The moon has her aspects of change in the skies,
  With her broad shield of silver, her crescent of gold,
But still there remains, turned away from our eyes,
  A part of her orb we can never behold.
Even such is our nature, yet do not despair,
  But foster kind feeling whatever befall ;
Wait, watch, and examine, with kindness and care,
  And grudge not the charity due unto all.

In outward demeanour, look, action and speech,
  We alter with circumstance, meaning no ill,
Unconsciously changing our manner to each,
  Through an instinct that prompteth the heart or the will
In the presence of some our affections rebel,
  With others our natural sympathies glow.

But the power which, by turns, doth attract and repel,
　　Is beyond what our limited wisdom can know.
Even such is our nature, but be of good cheer,
　　Nor let a first feeling your reason enthrall ;
Ye can be kind and truthful to those ye hold dear,
　　And still render charity due unto all.

How oft we encounter, from home-life apart,
　　The shy and forbidding, the frank and the bold !
But the sternest in face may be kindest at heart,
　　And the liveliest inwardly shallow and cold.
Yon stranger who seemeth all goodness and grace,
　　In worldly proprieties careful alway,
May be burning with passions that warp and debase,
　　And building up schemes to allure and betray.
Even such is man's nature, yet be ye not sad
　　That the light of his virtues seems fitful and small,
Acknowledge all good, make the best of the bad,
　　And thus render charity due unto all.

A false one may hail us in vesture of light,
　　And scatter with flowers the by-ways of wrong ;
A true one may haunt us in robes of the night,
　　And watch that we stumble not, passing along ;
One frowns in his virtues ; one smiles in his crimes,
　　One smites, while another uplifts from the ground ;
But our faith should be this—for we feel it sometimes—
　　That commixed with all evil some good may be found.
Then judge not too hastily, lest ye condemn,
　　And banish some angel ye cannot recall ;
To the firm of pure purpose, give honour to them,
　　To the frail give the charity due unto all.

THE HAPPY CHANGE.

(A TEMPERANCE RHYME.)

"OH ! will he come ?" said Alice Wray,
    " He did not *once* deceive,
      And for the dear sake of the past
        I will again believe."
So faithful Alice trimmed the hearth,
    And made the kettle sing,
Responsive to the cricket's voice
    That made the cottage ring.

Fair Alice and her children three,
    In clean, though poor attire,
Together chatted pleasantly
    Beside the evening fire.
Hark ! slowly beats the minster clock !
    Be patient yet awhile,
Another brief half hour, Alice,
    Will make thee weep or smile.

She waited with a throbbing heart
    Until the middle chime,
When William o'er the threshold stepped,
    Hours ere his wonted time.
Sober, erect, and thoughtful, too,
    He clasped his joyful wife,
Who deemed that sombre winter eve
    The happiest of her life.

" I 've vowed," he cried, " no more to touch
    The cup of deadly ill ;
God ! help me to retrieve the past
    With well-directed will !
And now, dear wife, let us partake
    The food which God has blessed."
And never was a frugal meal
    Enjoyed with sweeter zest.

With reverent hands he oped the Page
    He had not touched for years,
And read and wept, but found at last
    Hope, comfort, in his tears.
Then the contented pair lay down
    In peace, but newly won,
With the consoling consciousness
    Of one great duty done.

And William swerved not ; from that hour
    He chose the better way,
And from the path of usefulness
    Scarce had one thought to stray ;

With speech, heart, soul, he strove to wean
  The drunkard from his bane ;
Nor were his labours profitless,
  Nor were his teachings vain.

Few are the minds so prompt and firm
  As this once-erring one ;
Would there were more to help the frail,
  Ere every hope is gone !
Blest be the cause for which they toil,
  And may their power expand,
Till they have crushed the giant curse,
  The nightmare of the land !

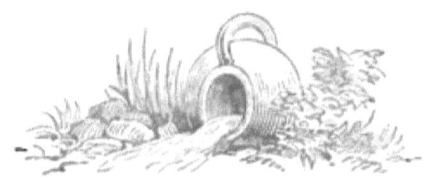

A VOICE FROM THE FACTORY.

(WRITTEN IN APRIL, 1851.)

I HEAR men laud the coming Exhibition,
   I read its promise in the printed page,
And thence I learn that its pacific mission
   Is to inform and dignify the age ;
It comes to congregate the alien nations,
   In new, but friendly bonds, old foes to bind ;
It comes to rouse to nobler emulations
   Man's skill of hand, man's energy of mind.

A thousand vessels breasting wind and ocean,
   A thousand fire-cars, snorting on their way,
Will startle London with a strange commotion,
   Beneath the genial radiance of May ;
And we shall hail the peaceable invasion
   With voice of welcome, cordial grasp of hand,
And, in the grandeur of the great occasion,
   See signs of brotherhood 'tween every land.

Would I might walk beneath that dome transcendent,
   Than old Alhambra's halls more proudly fair,
Nay, than Aladdin's palace more resplendent,
   Bright as if quarried from the fields of air ;
Would I might wander in its wondrous mazes,
   Filled with embodied thought in every guise,
See Art and Science in their countless phases,
   And bless the power that gave them to my eyes.

Men are about me with pale, vacant faces,
   Human in shape, in spirit dark and low ;
They do not care for Genius and its graces,
   Nor understand, nor do they seek to know.
But I have read and pondered, feeling ever
   Deep reverence for the lofty, good, and true,
And, therefore, yearn to see this high endeavour
   Stand grandly realised before my view.

But what to me are these inspiring changes,
   That gorgeous show, that spectacle sublime ?
My labour, leagued with poverty, estranges
   Me from this mental marvel of our time.
I cannot share the triumph and the pageant,
   I, a poor toiler at the whirling wheel,
The slave, not ruler, of a ponderous agent,
   With bounding steam-pulse, and with arms of steel.

My ears are soothed by no melodious measures,
   No work of sculptor charms my longing gaze,
No painter thrills me with exalted pleasures,
   But books and thought have cheered my darkest days.

E

Thank God for Sundays! Then impartial Nature
   Folds me within the shelter of her wings,
And drinking in her every voice and feature,
   I feel more reconciled to men and things.

I shall not see our Babel's summer wonder,
   Save in the proseman's page or poet's song,
But I shall hear it in the far-off thunder
   Of other lands, applauding loud and long.
Why should I murmur? I shall share with others
   The glorious fruits of that triumphant day;
Hail, to the time that makes all nations brothers!
   Hail, to the advent of the coming May!

HARVEST HYMN.

THE nations heave with throes of strife,
   And men look on with wondering eyes,
Mourn the dread waste of human life,
   Yet raise their angry battle-cries.
While poets cheer the valiant throng
   With chants of hope or victory,
Be mine a pure thanksgiving song,—
   Lord of the harvest, praise to Thee !

Thy tented fields how different they,
   How lovely, soothing, and serene !
Where the ripe sheaves, in long array,
   Smile in the soft autumnal sheen ;
And where no ruder sounds are heard
   Than the blithe reaper's voice of glee,
Or vagrant breeze, or gladsome bird,—
   Lord of the harvest, praise to Thee !

Whoever fails, Thou dost not fail ;
   Whoever sleeps, Thou dost not sleep ;
With fattening shower, and fostering gale,
   Thy mercy brings the time to reap ;

Man marks each season and its sign,
 And sows the seed and plants the tree,
But form, growth, fulness, all are Thine,—
 Lord of the harvest, praise to Thee !

O God ! it is a pleasant thing
 To see the precious grain expand,
And the broad hands of Plenty fling
 Her golden largess o'er the land ;
To see the fruitage swell and glow,
 And bow with wealth the parent tree ;
To see the purple vintage flow,—
 Lord of abundance, praise to Thee !

Praise for the glorious harvest days,
 And all the blessings that we share ;
For the unbounded sunlight praise,
 And for the free and vital air ;
Praise for the faith that looks above ;
 The hope of immortality ;
For life, health, virtue, truth and love,
 Maker and Giver, praise to Thee !

THE ARAB'S SONG.

IN Caypha's hallowed garden-grounds,
　　All shadowy, green and cool,
　Where leaps the living fountain-jet,
　　Where sleeps the glassy pool.
Swathed in an atmosphere of joy,
　There dwells a virgin flower,
Whose breath and beauty seem to fill
　Its consecrated bower.

The bulbul seems to love it, too,
　And pours its pensive tune
Through the soft lapse and slumbrous light
　Of the admiring moon ;
And when the morning kindleth up,
　The sun's enamoured beams
Look in to bless with fostering glow
　This flower of all my dreams.

The acacia drops its silver dew,
　The palm its tender gloom,
To cherish this " consummate flower,"
　And share its full perfume ;

Autumn Leaves.

And Syria's ardent sky looks down
  On its expanding form,
But seldom there hangs lowering cloud,
  Or wakes the voice of storm.

Its eyes, (oh, wild, yet winning eyes!)
  Which shame the proud gazelle,
Shine like twin trembling gems that lie
  In ocean's rosy shell.
Now they repose in quiet trance
  Beneath thought's holy sway;
Anon, they burn with haughty fire,
  To scare my hopes away.

So sweet its fragrance, and so far
  It floats on breeze and blast,
The pilgrim halts within its reach,
  And deems the desert passed,
The chief who flies on foaming steed
  Before unequal foes,
Checks for a space his fearful flight
  To breathe it as he goes.

The simoon's fleet and fiery wing
  Abhors all grateful smells,
And enters with its baneful power
  Where aught of freshness dwells;
But this one odour, closely sealed
  Within my faithful heart,
Outlives the weary, wasting wind,
  And will not thence depart.

The Arab's Song.

In the soft air of pastoral life,
  Away from griefs and glooms,
Untouched by sorrow, sin, or strife,
  This garden glory blooms.
Maiden, that blush of modest thought
  Reveals some hidden power,
Think of thy own dear, gentle name,
  And thou wilt know the flower.

Oh, 'twere a blessing lent of Heaven
  Through long enraptured years,
To watch, and shed around thee, too,
  Pure love's ecstatic tears !
My desert home, my tribe, my steed,
  My sword, my roving will,
I 'd yield them all with thee, sweet flower,
  To dwell on Carmel's hill !

HAPPY OLD AGE.

I FEEL that age has overta'en
　My steps on Life's descending way,
But Time has left no lingering pain,
　No shadow of an evil day ;
And you, my children, gather near
　To smooth and solace my decline,
And I have hope that your career
　Will be as blest as mine.

Not all exempt has been my sky
　From threatening storm and lowering cloud,
But sunbursts shed from source on high
　Have cheered my spirit when it bowed ;
Not all without the shard and thorn
　Has been my path, from first to last,
But springs and flowers, of Mercy born,
　Have soothed me as I passed.

I have not lived all free from sin,
　For what imperfect nature can ?
But I have no remorse within
　For scorn of my poor fellow-man ;

Kin to the humblest of my race,
    And 'bove all worldly sects and creeds,
I never turned disdainful face
    Against a brother's needs.

And now my mind, all clear and cool,
  . (As I serenely talk or muse,)
Is tranquil as yon glassy pool,
    Reflecting Autumn's sunset hues ;
Time has not dulled my moral sense,
    Nor has it dimmed my mental sight ;
No passions weaken my defence,
    No doubts and cares affright.

But Retrospection, even yet,
    Will lead me through past trodden ways,
And I remember—why forget ?
    The magic of my early days ;
All Nature so divinely wrought,
    The unravelled mystery of things,
Awoke me to exalted thought,
    And lent my spirit wings.

And I remember how I grew
    Up to the sunny noon of youth,
From youth to manhood, till I knew
    That love was near akin to truth.
My trials, bravely overcome ;
    My triumphs, not of purpose vain,
All these, with vague but pleasant hum
    Still murmur through my brain.

My children, offspring of a tree
　Whose top is hoary with decay,
Whose trunk is shaken as may be
　Before it falls and fades away—
Receive what faithful men unfold ;
　Revere what truthful men proclaim ;
And before Heaven and man uphold
　The honour of my name.

For me, I have no mortal fear,
　No tremblings as I hurry down,
My way is clear, the end is near,
　The goal, the glory, and the crown.
Then shed no bitter tears for me
　As ye consign me to the dust,
Rather rejoice that I shall be
　With God, my strength and trust.

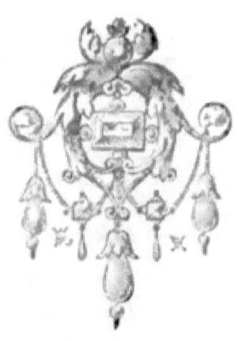

HYMN TO THE CREATOR.

(REPRINTED BY REQUEST.)

PRAISE unto God! whose single will and might,
  Upreared the boundless roof of day and night,
    With suns, and stars, and gorgeous cloud-wreaths
      hung,
The emblazoned veil that hides the Eternal's throne,
The glorious pavement of a world unknown,
  By angels trodden and by mortals sung!
To God! who fixed old ocean's utmost bounds,
And bade the moon, in her harmonious rounds,
  Govern its waters with her quiet smiles;
Bade the obedient winds, though seeming free,
Sweep the tumultuous surface of the sea,
  And place man's daring foot upon a thousand isles!

Praise unto God! who thrust the rifted hills,
With all their golden veins and gushing rills,
  Up from the burning centre long ago;
Who spread the deserts, verdureless and dun,
And those stern realms, forsaken of the sun,
  Where Frost has built his palace-halls of snow!

To God ! whose hands have anchored in the ground
The forest growth of ages, the profound
   Green hearts of solitude unsought of men !
God ! who suspends the avalanche ; who dips
The Alpine hollows in a cold eclipse,
   And hurls the headlong torrent shivering down the glen !

Praise unto God ! who speeds the lightning's wing
To fearful flight, making the thunder spring
   Abrupt and awful from its sultry lair,
To rouse some latent function of the earth,
To bring some natural blessing into birth,
   And sweep disorder from the lurid air!
To God ! who bids the hurricane awake,
The firm rock shudder, and the mountain quake,
   With deep and inextinguishable fires ;
Who urges ghastly pestilence to wrath,
And sends gaunt Famine on his silent path,
   The holy purpose hid from our profane desires !

Praise unto God ! who fills the fruitful soil
With wealth that waits the honest hand of Toil,
   With germs of beauty and abundance, too;
Who bends athwart the amplitude of skies
His braided sun-bow of resplendent dyes,
   Melting in rain-drops from the shadowy blue !
To God ! who sends the seasons, dark or bright !
Spring's constant resurrection of delight ;
   Summer's mature voluptuousness of mien ;
The generous flush of the Autumnal time ;
The-ever-changing spectacle sublime
   Of purgatorial Winter, savage or serene !

Praise unto God! whose wisdom placed me here,
A lowly dweller on this lovely sphere,
   This temporary home to mortals given;
Which holds its silent and unerring way
Among the innumerable worlds that stray,
   Shining and burning through the halls of heaven!
To God! who sent me hither to prepare,
By wordless worship, or by uttered prayer,
   By suffering, humanity, and love,
By sympathies and deeds from self apart,
Nursed by His gracious Spirit in the heart--
   For a transcendent life of purity above!

MAY.

MAY, May! song-honoured May!
Whom the youthful poet has loved alway,
What has become of thy genial air,
Thy voices of music everywhere,
The blessed blue of thy kindly skies,
Thy blooms that greet us with sweet surprise,
Thy hedgerows covered with odorous snow,
Thy waters that laugh with joy as they go?
Why art thou sullen and sad to-day,
   Song-honoured May?

May, May! ever-welcome May!
How strangely thou lookest on earth to-day,
Cloudy and tearful, cold and wild,
Like a petulant woman, or wayward child!
Has winter been striving to keep thee back?
Has his bullying gales waylaid thy track?
Or is there a change 'mid the stars sublime?
Or a fitful pause in the flight of time?
Thy name is here, but thy presence away,
   Ever-welcome May!

May, May! salubrious May!
We were wont to make merry thy natal day,
But custom, and feeling, are altered now,
And the people are changed even more than thou :
But we used to wander, in days of old,
Through fields of floral silver and gold,
Catching the apple-tree's breath and bloom,
And the ancient hawthorn's heavy perfume,
While our glad hearts beat with a healthful play
  Salubrious May!

But nothing goes wrong in the hands of God,
For His bounty lives in the quiet sod,
Whether clothed in the garb of frost or flower,
Or the liberal harvest's golden dower.
With a thoughtless spirit we oft complain,
But the doings of Nature are ne'er in vain,
For Wisdom governs the humblest things,
And Love o'ershadows with guardian wings ;
In God's just power there is no delay,
  O glorious May!

A SOUL IN SHADOW.

L O, a Soul in Shadow! shaken
       By the stormy winds of sin,
    By the draught of deadly fire!
By the wiser world forsaken,
    To the lowest herds akin,
       He has but one fierce desire.

One desire, to quench in madness
    Recollections dark and keen,
       Memories of the wasted past.
How can he feel touch of gladness,
    Brooding over what has been,
       While his conscience starts aghast?

Vain remorse! Behold his weakness
    'Mid the revel and the rout,
       Where dissolves his better will!
Where the host, with cunning sleekness,
    Hands the treacherous wine about,
       Or a draught more deadly still.

Now with mingled curse and clamour
   Drink's poor victims rouse the brawl,
     With wild brain and tainted breath ;
Sing, blaspheme, and reel and stammer,
   Reckless, ruthless, shameless all,
     'Mid the blazonry of death.

But the darkling Soul ! Oh, sorrow !
   How he struggles through the night
     Of a phantom-haunted sleep !
Till the sweet dawn of the morrow
   Shows his helplessness and blight !—
     Angels, ye have cause to weep !

Home has no regards and graces
   For this waif on Ruin's wild,
     And he seeks no solace there.
Wasted forms and gloomy faces
   Cannot make him reconciled
     To that dwelling of despair.

Yet, that Soul was once unclouded,
   Quick with intellectual fire,
     Dignified with moral power ;
Till the dread Temptation shrouded
   Hope, and peace, and pure desire,
     Which grew weaker every hour.

Exorcise him ! drive the Demon
   Out from his remorseful soul,
     Out from his unquiet heart !

F

Lift him up, a grateful freeman,
  With the means of self-control,
    And ye do a noble part !

Exorcise him ! not with preaching,
  Not with language harsh and cold,
    Not with looks of virtuous pride ;
But with Charity's mild teaching,
  With forgiveness manifold,
    Till his soul is purified.

England, old heroic nation !
  What avail thy lofty lore,
    Moral precepts, mighty words ?
Cleanse thee from this degradation,
  Which within thy sea-girt shore
    Slayeth more than all thy swords !

THE WASTE OF WAR.

GIVE me the gold that War has cost,
   In countless shocks of feud and fray,
  The wasted skill, the labour lost,
    The mental treasure thrown away,—
And I will buy each rood of soil
  In every yet discovered land,
Where hunters roam, where peasants toil,
  Where many-peopled cities stand.

I'll clothe each ragged wretch on earth
  In needful, yea, in brave attire,
Vesture befitting banquet mirth,
  Which kings might envy and admire.
In every vale, on every plain,
  A school shall glad the gazer's sight,
Where every poor man's child may gain
  Pure knowledge, free as air and light.

I'll build asylums for the poor,
  By age or ailment made forlorn ;
And none shall thrust them from the door,
  Or sting with looks and words of scorn.

I 'll link each alien hemisphere ;
　　Help honest men to conquer wrong ;
Art, Science, Labour, nerve and cheer ;
　　Reward the poet for his song.

In every crowded town shall rise
　　Halls Academic, amply graced,
Where ignorance may soon be wise,
　　And coarseness learn both art and taste.
To every province shall belong
　　Collegiate structures, and not few,
Filled with a truth-exploring throng,
　　With teachers of the good and true.

In every free and peopled clime
　　A vast Walhalla hall shall stand,
A marble edifice sublime
　　For the illustrious of the land ;
A pantheon for the truly great,
　　The wise, benevolent, and just !
A place of wide and lofty state
　　To honour or to hold their dust.

A temple to attract and teach
　　Shall lift its spire on every hill,
Where pious men shall feel and preach
　　Peace, mercy, tolerance, good-will.
Music of bells on Sabbath days
　　Round the whole earth shall gladly rise,
And one great Christian song of praise
　　Stream sweetly upward to the skies.

THE SUNDAY SCHOOL.

(WRITTEN FOR JUVENILES.)

THE people of our Christian land
Have cause to bless the men who planned
That place of gentle power and rule,
The noble British Sunday School;
For there the poor man's child may come,
As to a consecrated home,
And in its hallowed precincts find
Knowledge and comfort for the mind.

The man of toil has many a care,
And little, haply, can he spare,
To teach and elevate his child,
And keep its nature undefiled;
But here, whate'er his creed, or none,
His offspring will be looked upon
With kindly eyes, and shown the way
That opens into joyful day.

Some men of toil, though husbands, sires,
May cherish selfish, low desires,

And waste the means which, wisely spent,
Would bring their household calm content.
Or they may be—how sad the case !—
In language rude, of manners base,
And by a false and fierce control
Corrupt the young untutored soul.

Then more the need that there should be
This refuge of humanity,
Where *one* day, richest of the seven,
The child may learn of love and Heaven.
But if the mother does not feel
For moral and religious weal ;
If all her better instincts sleep,
Well may the pitying angels weep !

'Tis pleasant on a Sabbath morn,
When music on the air is borne,
To see young children, trim and neat,
Come forth from many a crowded street,
From mountain side, and vale and lea,
Where'er their dwelling-place may be,
To seek the Sunday School again,
Their own unbought and free domain.

And is it not a joy, I ask,
To hear them at the holy task,
Like bees assiduous in the hive,
Hoarding the sweets on which they thrive ?
Seeking to know, and know aright,
The sacred Word, the Gospel light,

The glorious Gospel, which has power
To cheer the Christian's darkest hour.

'Tis grand on some great Holiday
To see their orderly array,
Marshalled by zealous men, whose pride
Is to be with them, side by side.
They go to spend a day of joy
Unmingled with the world's alloy,
In Nature's presence to adore,
And learn from God one lesson more.

They seek the woodland's slumbrous shade
Which the fierce sun can scarce invade,
Where, banquet done, and prayer preferred,
The foliage of the trees is stirred
With a thanksgiving hymn of power,
That sanctifies that sylvan bower,
Whilst angels, listening with glad eyes,
Call the song upward to the skies.

This day will serve them through the year
With thoughts of pleasantness and cheer,
Enhance their love of harmless things,
And quicken young Devotion's wings.
Ye careful parents, when ye find
Good seed sown in the youthful mind,
Foster its growth with all your power,
And bring it into beauteous flower.

O Sunday Schools ! O Christian land !
Long may your institutions stand,

The wonder of the farthest zone,
The strength and glory of your own !
Be this the Sabbath teacher's prayer,
For those beneath his watchful care, .
" Father, thy countless flock behold,
And bring them safely to Thy fold."

THE HOUSEHOLD, JEWELS.

(REPRINTED BY REQUEST.)

A TRAVELLER, from journeying
  In countries far away,
    Repassed his threshold at the close
      Of one blest Sabbath day ;
A comely face, a voice of love,
  A kiss of chaste delight,
Were the first things to welcome him
  On that sweet Sabbath night.

He stretched his limbs upon the hearth,
  Before its friendly blaze,
And conjured up mixed memories
  Of gay and gloomy days,
Feeling that none of gentle soul,
  However far he roam,
Can e'er forego, can e'er forget
  The tranquil joys of home.

" Bring me my children," cried the sire,
 With eager, earnest tone.
" I long to press them, and to mark
 How lovely they have grown.
Twelve weary months have passed away
 Since I went o'er the sea,
To feel how sad and lone I am
 Without my babes and thee."

" Refresh thee, as 'tis needful," said
 The fair and faithful wife,
The while her pensive features paled,
 And stirred with inward strife.
" Refresh thee, husband of my heart,
 I ask it as a boon ;
Our children are reposing, love,
 Thou shalt behold them soon."

She spread the meal, she filled the cup,
 And pressed him to partake ;
He sat down blithely at the board,
 And all for her sweet sake ;
But when the frugal meal was done,
 The thankful prayer preferred,
Again Affection's fountain flowed,
 Again its voice was heard.

" Bring me my children, darling wife,
 I 'm in a genial mood,
My soul wants purer aliment,
 I crave for other food ;

Bring forth my children to my gaze,
　Or ere I rage or weep ;
I yearn to kiss their happy eyes
　Before the hour of sleep."

" I have a question yet to ask,
　Be patient, husband dear :
A stranger one auspicious morn
　•Did send some jewels here,
Until, to take them from my care,
　But yesterday he came,
And I restored them, with a sigh ;
　Dost thou approve, or blame ? "

" I marvel much, sweet wife, that thou
　Shouldst breathe such words to me ;
Repay to man, resign to God,
　Whate'er is lent to thee ;
Restore it with a willing heart,
　Be grateful for the trust ;
Whate'er may tempt or try us, wife,
　Let us be ever just."

She took him by the passive hand,
　And up the moonlit stair
She led him to a snow-white bed,
　With mute and mournful air ;
She turned the cover down, and there,
　In grave-like garments dressed,
Lay the twin children of their love,
　In death's serenest rest.

" These were the jewels lent to me,
 Which God has deigned to own ;
The precious caskets still remain,
 But, ah, the *gems* are gone !
But thou didst teach me to resign
 What God alone can claim ;
He giveth, and He takes away,
 Blest be His holy name ! "

The father gazed upon his babes,
 The mother drooped apart,
While all the woman's sorrow gushed
 From her o'erburdened heart ;
And with the striving of her grief,
 Which wrung the tears she shed,
Were mingled low and loving words
 To the unconscious dead.

When the sad sire had looked his fill,
 He veiled each breathless face,
And down in self-abasement bowed,
 For comfort and for grace ;
With the deep eloquence of woe
 Poured forth his secret soul,
Rose up, and stood erect and calm,
 In spirit healed and whole.

" Restrain thy tears, poor wife," he said,
 " I learn this lesson still,
That God who gives can take away,
 Blest be His holy will !

Blest are our children, for they *live*
 From sin and sorrow free,
And I am not all joyless, wife,
 With faith, hope, love, and thee."

MY FRIENDS OF CHORLEY.

THE earth lay entranced in the glories of June,
  The flowers were in splendour, the birds were in tune,
  When I, a poor wayfarer, plodded along,
Surrounded by beauty, and fragrance, and song ;
But weary and hungry, in quest of employ,
My soul could not mingle with Nature's great joy.
Till at length I encountered a friend by the way,—
A friend I had known in a happier day—
And he without coldness, or question, or guile,
Gave the bread and the cup, with a kind word and smile ;
And more, for he stirred other hearts to my need,
And their aid and their sympathy cheered me indeed.

  I shall ever remember that sociable night,
When my friends gathered round me to help and delight ;
Honest men and hard-workers, a right pleasant throng,
Who could feel for the bard, while they honoured his song.
How quickly and cheerfully passed the brief time,
With the bountiful mixture of reason and rhyme,
With the good-natured banter, which gave no offence,
With the laugh of good-humour, the speech of good sense
With song, recitation, and other good things,
Which sped the brief hours on delectable wings :

And more than all this, there was mixed with the whole,
A feeling which touched and exalted the soul.

And who shall presume to discourage with scorn
The brave son of toil, with his duties o'erworn,
Who seeks to enjoy, in a rational way,
The small leisure left him throughout the long day ?
Not I ; for dear freedom, in action and mind,
When used with right reason, and justly defined,
Is the claim of all men, yea, their claim and their need,
And the stark son of labour deserves it indeed.

Dear friends, newly found, I will try to retain
Your hearty good-will till I meet you again,
And may our next meeting come gladly and soon,
And may fickle Fortune just grant me a boon,
That I may reward you, with feelings of glee,
For the delicate aid that you rendered to me.

Let us give when we can, for to give is to gain,
As the earth gets her own exhalations in rain ;
Each free gift of charity goes to increase,
And returns to us sweetly to bless us with peace ;
Let us foster kind feeling in this world of ours,
For such is the " odour of heavenly flowers."

Fellow workers, 'twere vain my rude verse to prolong,
For I cannot tell *all* my emotions in song,
But I'll cherish your memory, happen what may,
Whate'er be my fortune, for many a day ;
May your blessings be many, your sorrows be few,
May health, peace, and virtue befriend you !   Adieu !

A PRAYER FOR PEACE.

PEACE for the nations, God,
   For the harassed earth complains
   That her sons are defiling the fertile sod
      With the blood of each other's veins ;
And sounds of rage and regret are rife ;
And men grow mad 'mid the waste of life ;
Labour's broad brow grows furrowed and pale,
And homes are disturbed with the voice of wail,
And fast coming griefs, bewildering fears,
From countless hearts wring curses and tears ;
While the spirit of Progress back recoils
At the far-borne bruit of unhallowed broils,
And Freedom shudders with strange dismay,
As she veils her face from the light of day !
Restore to us Peace, a transcendent dower,
If such be the will of Thy holy power.

Peace for the houschold, Lord !
   Let each unto each so cling,
That all may appear in a bright accord,
   Like pearls on a golden string.

Let love be the sweet and presiding grace
To charm into beauty the dwelling-place ;
To soften the language of firm command,
And lighten the cares of the household band ;
To mould the heart with a delicate stress,
And wake its emotions of tenderness ;
To train the mind to exalted things,
And lift the soul upon skyward wings ;
Peace for the hearth, and the purest air,
That thought may burst into constant prayer,
Into silent worship, serenely rife
'Mid the duties and pains of mortal life,
That earth may grow on her changeful sod
Immortal blooms for Thy gardens, God !

WHITTLE SPRINGS.

(A REMINISCENCE.)

RESPECTFULLY INSCRIBED TO THOMAS HOWARD, ESQ., OF HYDE,
OWNER OF THE ESTATE.

IT was a Summer's gorgeous eventide,
  Softly and sweetly silent, warm and bright,
And all the breadth of glorious landscape wide
  Was swathed in vesture of serenest light;
When with a friend I took my pleasant way
To an old shadowy, sylvan nook, that lay
A league apart from any street and town,
In a romantic valley, hushed and brown.
Our winding pathway led through lonely lanes,
Now busy with the fragrant harvest wains,
Where banks of plume-like fern grew thick and green,
Where groups of foxgloves stood with stately mien
On grassy slopes, and in the vagrant breeze
Shook all their wealth of crimson chalices.
From shadowy brake and wavering bough was heard
The frequent voice of some unsettled bird;
The limber honeysuckle seemed to sigh
Unto the clustering wild rose lovingly,

And both sent through the calm and verdant gloom
The mingled breathings of their rich perfume.

We entered by a low and Gothic gate
Into a sweet retreat of fairy state,—
A lone and lovely spot, that smiled at rest
On the green valley's ever-quiet breast ;
A refuge quaint of chequered light and shade,
All cunningly and beautifully made
By art and nature's harmonising power
Into an intricate and magic bower ;
Embroidered everywhere with richest dyes,
And curtained o'er with soft and cloudless skies ;
Encircled with a zone of beauteous things,
A place of pleasure, welcome Whittle Springs !

With loitering feet we traced the cultured grounds,
And calmly listened to the various sounds
Of childish gladsomeness and youthful glee,
And ballad strains of ancient melody.
We watched the athletic bowlers on the green,
As a great billiard-table smooth and clean ;
Stopped to regard a troop of merry boys,
Holding their pastime with obstreperous noise ;
Wound through the verdant mazes of the brake
All richly redolent with rarest flowers,
Bright forms of full perfume, that sweetly spake
Of southern climates and their gorgeous bowers.

We paused a while beside the tranquil pool,
Ample in breadth, pellucid, bright and cool,

Scarce ruffled by the graceful moving pair
Of snowy swans that idly floated there ;
And then, with honour to the place, we quaffed
A doubly copious and refreshing draught
From the twin Springs, whose ever-healthful powers
Bring cheerful thousands to their pleasant bowers.

But now the sinking Sun-god paused to rest
On the bright borders of the purpling west,
While hill and vale, and distant copse and glade
Began to gather into deeper shade,
And we withdrew within, intent to spend
A pleasant hour with stranger and with friend
In sweet and social converse, such as binds
In peaceful union true hearts and minds.
Within the lofty and antique saloon,
   With many-coloured windows gaily dight,
We sat and watched the now ascending moon
   Pour in the sweetness of her mellow light ;
And we beheld with mute but glad surprise
Things which enchant the silent gazer's eyes,
A hundred shapes and hues of pictured grace,
The healthful bloom of many a lovely face,
And sculptured forms, majestical and fair,
Which give the whole a chaste and classic air ;
Beauties that make us half forget that we
   Are near the murky realm of noisy trade,
And make us glad that we can quickly be
   Where its rude sounds cannot our ears invade.
O Whittle Springs ! thou art a pleasant spot,
Where human sorrow may be half forgot.

A tranquil refuge of serene delight
To those made weary in the world's rude fight ;
A place of quiet or of stirring joy,
Where harassed minds may find some sweet employ !
The thoughtful penman leaves his books and care
To find some calm and cheerful solace there ;
The weary worker cometh from the town ;
The wayward painter puts his pencil down,
And cometh here in quest of newer themes ;
The poet cometh to refresh his dreams ;
For song, and dance, and temperate feast and wine,
And forms of beauty which seem half divine,
And pleasant smiles, and laughter beaming eyes,
Make thee at times a social paradise,
And still my fond and faithful memory clings
To thy serene delights, famed Whittle Springs !*

* This secluded spot of resort, and harmless recreation, is becoming daily
more popular. In addition to its medicinal springs, it possesses charms of a
varied character. Art has combined with nature in rendering it a place
pleasant to visit and remember. The proprietor of the grounds has spared
no pains and expense in providing for the pleasure and comfort of his
visitors. To the people of Blackburn, Preston, Chorley, and neighbour-
hoods, there are cheap facilities of reaching it. Altogether, Whittle Springs
is worthy the patronage of any class, and a most attractive and desirable
place of resort for the toiling community of Lancashire. May it meet with
that support it so highly deserves.

HUMAN BROTHERHOOD.

THE king who is swathed in the splendours of state,
　　Whose power and possessions are wide,
　　Is akin to the beggar who whines at his gate,
　Howe'er it may torture his pride ;
He is subject to ailments, and dangers, and woes,
　As the wretch who encounters the blast,
And despite of his grandeur, his bones must repose
　In the same grave of nature at last.

The beauty, surrounded by homage and wealth,
　Whose glance of command is supreme,
Who walks in the grace of rich raiment and health,
　Whose life seems a musical dream,
Is sister to her who, old, haggard and worn,
　Receives a chance crust by the way ;
The proud one may treat her with silence and scorn,
　But their kinship no truth can gainsay.

The scholar who glories in gifts of the mind,
　Who ransacks the treasures of Time,
Who scatters his thoughts on the breath of the wind,
　And makes his own being sublime,

Even he is a brother to him at the plough,
  Whose feet crush the flowers in their bloom ;
And to him who toils on with a care-furrowed brow
  In chambers of clangour and gloom.

Chance, circumstance, intellect, change us in life,
  Repulse us and keep us apart,
But would we had less of injustice and strife,
  And more of right reason and heart.
One great human family, born of one Power,
  Each claiming humanity's thought,
We should let our best sympathies flow like a dower,
  And give and receive as we ought.

BROAD CAST THY SEED.

B ROAD cast thy seed ;
    If thou hast aught of wealth to lend,
      Beyond what reason bids thee spend,
Seek out the haunts of want and woe,
And let thy bounty wisely flow ;
Lift modest merit from the dust,
And fill his heart with joy and trust ;
Take struggling genius by the hand,
And bid his striving soul expand ;
Where virtuous men together cling,
To vanquish some unhallowed thing,
Join the just league, and not withhold
Thy heart, thy counsel, and thy gold ;
Thus to achieve some noble deed,
    Broad cast thy seed.

    Broad cast thy seed ;
If thou hast *mind,* thou hast to spare,
And giving may increase thy share ;
Pour forth thy thought with friendly zeal,
And make some stubborn spirit feel

The grace, the glory, the delight,
That spring from knowledge used aright ;
The improving wealth, which none can take,
Though fortune fly, and friends forsake ;
The mental vision, more and more
Expanding as he dares to soar.
Virtue and knowledge, glorious twain !
The more they give the more they gain !
Wouldst have thy humbler brother freed ?
   Broad cast thy seed.

   Broad cast thy seed ;
Although some portion may be found
To fall on uncongenial ground,
Where sand, or shard, or stone may stay
Its coming into light of day,
Or when it comes, some pestilent air
May make it droop and wither there,
Be not discouraged ; some may find
Congenial soil, and gentle wind,
Refreshing dew and ripening shower,
To bring it into beauteous flower,
From flower to fruit, to glad thy eyes,
And fill thy soul with sweet surprise.
Do good, and God will bless thy deed ;
   Broad cast thy seed !

A POET'S WISH.

(REPRINTED BY REQUEST.)

OH! give me a cot in some wood-shaded glen,
   Shut in from the clangour of conflict and pain,
  Far away from the turmoil of town-prisoned men,
  Who strive for subsistence and struggle for gain.
Secure from intrusion, aloof from annoy,
   My chiefest companions my wife and my child,
I could think with some purpose, and labour with joy,
   In that home of seclusion, far, far in the wild.

The lark should arouse me to action and thought;
   I would take my first draught at the health-giving rill;
I would gaze on the beauties that morning had brought,
   As I strengthened my limbs up the slope of the hill.
The early prayer uttered, the early meal done,
   The day should have uses and joys undefiled;
Some good should be gathered, some knowledge be won,
   In that home of seclusion, far, far in the wild.

When the clouds which were golden grew faint in the
    west,
  The sun having left them to melt in the sky ;
When Nature seemed folding her mantle for rest,
  And Hesperus hung his bright cresset on high,
I would draw up my household about the fireside,
  (Unless the dear Muses my fancy beguiled,)
To talk with and teach them, with pleasure and pride,
  In that home of seclusion, far, far in the wild.

I would have, would kind Fortune her bounty impart,
  Nor blind me to virtue, nor steel me to woe—
Some good thing and graceful in nature and art ;
  Some music to make my best feelings o'erflow ;
Some touch of the Painter to gladden my eyes ;
  Some books, to enchant my dark cares till they
    smiled ;
Some shape of the Sculptor, to charm and surprise,
  In that home of seclusion, far, far in the wild.

Surrounded by Nature, I could not but see
  In each change of season God's goodness unworn ;
For Spring would delight with bloom, beauty, and glee,
  The Summer with hay-harvest, Autumn with corn ;
Even Winter would charm me, though savage and cold,
  With his frost-work fantastic, his snow-drifts uppiled,
With his phalanx of storm-clouds, arrayed and unrolled
  O'er that home of seclusion, far, far in the wild.

I would blend with benevolence nothing austere,
  To the wayward be calm, to the worthy be kind,

I would give to the mourner some comfort and cheer,
   And waken some hope in the gloomiest mind ;
Thus earnest and helping, confiding and just,
   I should get my reward from a Source undefiled,
With assurance of mercy go down to the dust
   In that home of seclusion, far, far in the wild.

THE "NEW YEAR."

THE poet sings of many things
    In lands, and seas, and skies,
    As Fancy's many-coloured wings
Flutter before his eyes ;
But I, who love the tuneful throng,
    And hold the Muses dear,
Offer an unpretending song
    To hail the Glad New Year.

Again has come the festive time,
    Which holds us in control,
Morn of a mystery sublime
    Linked with the human soul ;
We serve with hospitable care
    Our daintiest Christmas cheer,
Grow free and friendly, and prepare
    To hail the Glad New Year.

Now is the season to forgive
    The wayward and unkind,
Let the heart's best emotions live
    To purify the mind ;

To let the memory retrace
    Our fitful past career,
To look the future in the face,
    And hail the Glad New Year.

Sorrows and losses we have borne,
    Been baffled and dismayed,
And felt the prick of many a thorn
    By our own follies made ;
But hope and effort may improve
    What now seems most severe,
If we begin with earnest love,
    And hail the Glad New Year.

Let us be thankful that God's power
    Has spared us yet a while,
Strive to enjoy the present hour,
    And make the future smile ;
Let us with charity and peace
    Make life more calm and clear,
Pray that discordant things may cease,
    As dawns the Glad New Year.

The sad old year is waning fast,
    And we are fading too,
But let our minds not stand aghast
    At what remains to do ;
Good will to all ! may joy prevail
    In homes both far and near,
And hope inspire us as we hail
    The gracious, Glad New Year.

HOPE AND PERSEVERANCE.

STRIVE on, brave souls, and win your way
　　By energy and care,
　Waste not one portion of the day
　In languor or despair ;
A constant drop will wear the stone,
　A constant effort clear
Your way, however wild and lone—
　Hope on and persevere.

Strive on, and if a shadow fall
　To dim your forward view,
Think that the sun is over all,
　And will shine out anew ;
Disdain the obstacles ye meet,
　And to one course adhere,
Advance with quick but cautious feet
　Hope on and persevere,

Rough places may deform the path
　That ye desire to tread,

And clouds of mingled gloom and wrath
　May threaten overhead,
Voices of menace and alarm
　May startle ye with fear,
But faith has a prevailing charm—
　Believe and persevere.

FORGIVENESS.

MY heart was galled with bitter wrong,
   Revengeful feelings fired my blood ;
  I cherished hate with passion strong,
   While round my couch dark demons stood.
Kind slumber wooed my eyes in vain,
   My burning brain conceived a plan—
"Revenge!" I cried in frantic strain ;
   But conscience whispered, "Be a man !"

"Forgive," a gentle spirit cried ;
   I yielded to my nobler part,
Uprose, and to my foeman hied,
   And then forgave him from my heart.
The big tears from their fountains rose,
   He melted—vowed my friend to be ;
That night I sank in sweet repose,
   And dreamed that angels smiled on me.

RANDOM RHYMES.

LET stand-still souls bemoan the dreary past,
　　With all its errors numberless and vast ;
　　Its waste in warfare, torture-tools, and fires,
Its false ambitions and its fierce desires,
Its clouded intellects and fettered tongues,
Its rank intolerance and its lawless wrongs,
Its savage serfdom and its sordid power,
Its horrors fearful as delirium's hour,
Its cruel codes and desolating crimes,
Unlike the triumphs of our later times.
These peaceful unions of the great and small,
That crowd and dignify this spacious hall ;
These proofs of progress, these inspiring sights,
That give us hope of loftier delights ;
These signs and promises of things that throng
The prophet's vision, and the poet's song—
Shadows that seem, but shadows that shall grow
To bright and blest realities below.
　　Onward, still onward, with assiduous speed,
And be your efforts equal to your need ;

Linger not, languish not, in march nor mind,
Nor stay to look upon the plain behind ;
One footstep lost, another gains the race,
And leaves you toiling in a backward place.
Onward, still onward, with unshrinking soul,
Your children follow and shall win the goal,
Shall win the guerdon of your toils, and stray
Within the opening dawn of Freedom's perfect day.
  Workers that weary in the mill and mine,
Come to the banquet, which is half divine ;
Craftsmen that labour at the bench and stall,
The door is open and the cost is small ;
Shopmen who sicken with the cares of trade,
Seek the Lyceum for your solace made ;
Magnates who struggle with unwieldy wealth,
Fly to our refuge for your spirits' health.
All, all are welcome, be they high or low,
We 've food for laughter, we have balm for woe.
Go on rejoicing, steadfast in the right,
Increasing still in intellectual might,
And I, a unit in the worldly throng,
Will wake my lowly harp, and cheer your way with
    song.

AT MY WIFE'S GRAVE SIDE.

SIX years have passed, my loved lost wife,
　　Since thou wast taken from my breast,
　　And cradled in thy final rest,
Leaving me lone with grief and strife.

And now I stand upon the sward
　　That vails thy simple burial-place ;
　　And with a pale and drooping face,
Survey it with a sad regard.

And as I gaze sweep through my brain
　　Things of the past on wings of gloom,
　　So that the mosses on thy tomb
Are watered by my tears of pain.

I see thee in the strength of youth,
　　With beauty in thy face and form,
　　With all thy feelings pure and warm,
Thy language sweet with artless truth.

Again I see thee sorely tried
  Beneath an overwhelming cloud —
  Thy freshness gone, thy spirit bowed
By poverty's dark ills allied.

I see thee in that troublous hour
  When death smote down our darling child,
  Made thee disconsolate and wild,
And me o'erawed by his dread power.

'Mid all I found thee wholly true
  Unto thy offspring and to me.
  May God, who set thy spirit free,
Console and strengthen me anew.

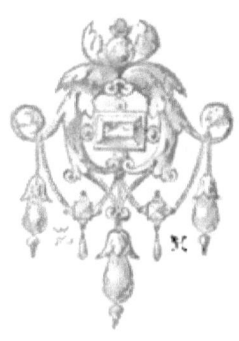

THE POSTMAN.

THE Postman is the people's man,
  Ready of foot and eye and hand,
  Who bears a blessing or a ban
To many in the land.
But whether he bring hope or dread,
  Tending to make me rich or poor,
As he so bravely earns his bread,
  He 's welcome at my door.

With muttered word and smothered sigh
  We look and listen for his feet,
And watch him with a wary eye
  As he comes down the street.
But if I dwell in field or town,
  Upon a mud or marble floor,
Whether my fortune smile or frown,
  He 's welcome at my door.

The statesman bent on lofty schemes,
  Good for the people or the throne ;
The poet weaving pleasant dreams,
  Alike the Postman own.

He lends the lover's mind new wings,
  In crowded mart, on lonely moor ;
And though he brings me few good things,
  He 's welcome at my door.

He braves the time, whate'er it be,
  The stormy wind, the hail, the shower,
And leaves his words of grief or glee
  At the appointed hour.
He bears his missives morn and eve
  Alike unto the rich and poor,
But if he make me glad or grieve,
  He 's welcome at my door.

He scatters wide the printed page,
  Filled with the various thoughts of men,
For much does our inquiring age
  Owe to the press and pen.
He brings the book to teach and please
  The ever-toiling, patient poor ;
And while he offers things like these,
  He 's welcome at my door.

When comes the Christmas holiday
  Let 's not forget this herald true,
But strive to help his scanty pay
  By some free gift that 's due.
He wakes strange feelings in the breast
  Of proud patrician, squire, or boor ;
And whether he make or mar my rest,
  He 's welcome at my door.

THE WORKMAN TO HIS WIFE.

DEAR wife, we struggle in a time
　　Saddened by many a shade,
For warfare in another clime
　Has paralysed my trade ;
And 'mong the thousands of our class,
　So meanly clothed and fed,
We 've had our share of grief, alas !
　Pining for needful bread.

But let us not relax, and fret
　As if all hope were gone ;
Let us not murmur and forget
　The all-sustaining One.
His is the justice, His the power
　To chasten and subdue ;
But even in the gloomiest hour
　His mercy shineth through.

Together let us strive to bear,
　With resolute calm will,
The burden of our daily care,
　Hoping and trusting still.

As we are human, we must feel
  Our portion of distress ;
But working with a righteous zeal
  Should make our trouble less.

Being but human, we must show
  Some frailties and some.fears,
Blindly creating needless woe,
  And shedding needless tears.
But, O my wife ! let thee and me
  Refrain from foolish strife,
And so behave that we may be
  Heirs to a holier life.

Of sorrow we must bear our part
  While in this lower sphere,
But let us keep a loving heart,
  And hold each other dear.
Though poverty may keep us down,
  Making us sad the while,
Let us not dare God's awful frown,
  But pray to gain His smile.

THE RETURN OF SPRING.

HOW calm and how beneficent is God
   To all His creatures in this world of ours !
   Spring is returned with renovating powers,
To clear the sky, and fertilise the sod,
To make the expanded landscape greenly bright,
And fill the genial air with music and delight.

I, like a weather-beaten plant, have grown
   Seedy and frail, the sport of every wind ;
   Yet in my daily watchfulness I find,
That in my weakness I am not alone—
Not an exception in the general plan,
But a still hopeful, striving, sinful, sorrowing man.

I long to wander where the old hills stand,
   And where the woods will soon grow newly green—
   To mark the silent changes of the scene,
Made by the hallowed touch of God's own hand—
To see the resurrection and the life
Of countless earthly things with strength and beauty rife.

I long to see the blithe lark soaring high,
   And the sweet thrush on his accustomed tree—
   To hear the loosened waters flowing free
Through places pleasant to the poet's eye—

To hear the murmur of the odorous breeze,
And the responsive sigh of congregated trees—

To hear the sportive children here and there
  In lonely hamlets nestled in the vales—
  To hear the aged people telling tales
Of their own youth when everything was fair—
To hear the voices of great nature raise
A simultaneous hymn of thankfulness and praise.

What sinless pleasure to explore again '
  The fields bestarr'd with daisies far and wide—
  The slender king-cup in its graceful pride
Holding its golden chalice for the rain—
The cowslip's bell, the dandelion's shield,
Lending their mingled hues to beautify the field.

What peaceful joy to find in woodland shades
  The modest violet bespent with dews,
  The fragrant primrose with its dainty hues,
And other floral sisters of the glades ;
Birds, leaves, and flowers, colours and perfumes,
And all the rich array of spring's ambrosial blooms.

Lord and Creator of these wondrous things,
  Oh ! grant me health, that I may feel once more
  Thy love and wisdom, as I felt of yore,
When I had many thoughts without their stings.
Oh ! spare and strengthen me a little time,
That I may worship Thee, and read Thy works sublime.

THE SONGS OF THE PEOPLE.

OH ! the Songs of the People are voices of power
  That echo in many a land ;
    They lighten the heart in the sorrowful hour,
  And quicken the labour of hand ;
They gladden the shepherd on mountain and plain,
  And the mariner tossed on the sea.
The poets have given us many a strain,
  But the Songs of the People for me.

The artizan, wending full early to toil,
  Sings a snatch of old song by the way ;
The ploughman, who sturdily furrows the soil,
  Cheers the morn with the words of his lay ;
The man at the stithy, the maid at the wheel,
  The mother with babe on her knee,
Chant simple old rhymes, which they tenderly feel.
  Oh ! the Songs of the People for me.

An anthem of triumph, a ditty of love,
  A carol 'gainst sorrow and care,

A hymn of the household that rises above,
  In the music of hope or despair ;
A strain patriotic that wakens the soul
  To all that is noble and free ;
These lyrics o'er men have a stirring control.
  Oh ! the Songs of the People for me.

THE END.

Manchester: Abel Heywood & Son, Printers.

www.ingramcontent.com/pod-product-compliance
Lightning Source LLC
Chambersburg PA
CBHW031157050726
47495CB00019B/2352